Jungle Book

MAGNA BOOKS

One warm evening, Shere Khan, a ferocious Indian tiger, was prowling around the jungle.

"Begone!" snarled a pack of wolves. "This is our hunting ground." No one had seen the human baby crawling on the ground.

Shere Khan sauntered away; he was not in the mood for a fight.

The wolves heard a chuckling, and turned to see the man-child.

"Who would abandon such a child?" said Mother Wolf, licking the baby like one of her own.

"We will just have to adopt him," replied Father Wolf. "I suggest we name him Mowgli."

When Bagheera, the panther, heard the news she offered to help rear the man-child. And Baloo, the bear, agreed to teach Mowgli the laws of the jungle.

As the years passed, Mowgli grew strong and agile. Baloo and Bagheera, between them, taught him to swim and to climb, to hunt and to protect himself from the dangers of the jungle.

One hot and sultry night, Shere Khan came to challenge Mowgli. "You do not belong in the jungle. Leave or I will kill you."

Mowgli was not in the least frightened. "I will leave if my brothers so wish. But not before I have slain you," he answered bravely.

With a torch of fire lit from the embers, Mowgli
successfully drove Shere Khan away.
"But he won't be gone for long," he thought.

Mowgli often spent his evenings high up in a tree, listening to the village elders talking. He soon discovered that they too were being terrorised by Shere Khan. The tiger was attacking their sheep and goats.

It was time to act! At the head of a herd of buffalo, Mowgli went in search of the tiger.

Shere Khan was sleeping in the long grass, when the buffalo, catching his scent on the wind, stampeded. He was surrounded, and before the tiger could escape he was trampled to death.

Mowgli had not only outwitted his enemy, he had saved the village and the jungle from the ravages of a savage tiger!

He was no longer a boy. Mowgli had become a man, respected by all who lived in the jungle.

Published by Magna Books   © 1993 Twin Books Ltd
Magna Road
Wigston
Leicester LE18 4ZH   Directed by CND – Muriel Nathan-Deiller
                     Illustrated by Van Gool-Lefévre-Loiseaux
                     Story adapted by Sue Jackson

Produced by
TWIN BOOKS LTD   All rights reserved.
Kimbolton House
117A Fulham Road   ISBN 1 85422 504 9
London SW3 6RL
                   Printed in Italy